Pokémon

I Feel Skitty!

**Adapted by Tracey West
and Katherine Noll**

SCHOLASTIC INC.

New York   Toronto   London   Auckland   Sydney
Mexico City   New Delhi   Hong Kong   Buenos Aires

Published by Scholastic Inc.
90 Old Sherman Turnpike, Danbury, CT 06816.

ISBN 0-439-72199-7

First Scholastic Printing, August 2005

"Great job, Beautifly!" May cried. May was training her new Beautifly. She wanted to enter it in a Pokémon Contest.

May threw a flying disc at Beautifly. It was practicing its Gust move. But May threw the disc too far.

"Would you mind getting that for me, Torchic?" May asked.

The little Fire Pokémon ran after the disc.

But Torchic did not come back.
May and the others went to look for
it. They found the disc, but did not
see Torchic.

Then they heard a noise in
the grass.

"Let's go look," said Brock.

They found Torchic in the grass--with another Pokémon!

"What is that?" Ash asked. He used his Pokédex to find out.

"Skitty, the Kitten Pokemon," the Pokédex said. "Skitty likes to chase anything that moves!"

"You are so cute!" May said to Skitty. "I have to catch you!"

But Skitty did not move.

May picked up the Pokémon. "I think it is sick," said May.

Brock tried to feed Skitty some special Pokémon food. But Skitty would not eat it.

May was worried. "Something is wrong with Skitty," she said.

"I have an idea," Brock said. "We can take Skitty to the Pokémon aromatherapy lab. They use Sweet Scent from Oddish and Weepinbell to make fragrances that heal Pokémon."

Brock took them to the lab.
They met a woman named Eliza who
worked there.

"We do use Sweet Scent," Eliza
said. "Then we mix it with all kinds
of herbs and mints. The smell makes
sick Pokémon feel better."

Eliza looked at Skitty.

"Will Skitty be okay?" asked May.

"I think Skitty is just tired!" Eliza said. "I will make a healing mix that will help Skitty while it rests."

While Eliza worked, Team
Rocket spied on the lab from
their balloon.

"Let's steal some of those sweet
smells," Jessie said. "We can use
them to heal our Pokémon."

Back in the lab, Eliza made a mix for Skitty. The healing mix made the Kitten Pokémon sleepy.

Finally, Skitty woke up. It started to chase its tail.

"You did it Eliza," May said. "Skitty is all better!"

Skitty wanted to play with
Pikachu. It chased after Pikachu's tail.
"Piiiiiiiika!" cried Pikachu. It tried
to run away.

May threw out a Poké Ball and said, "Time to catch that Skitty!"

Torchic popped out. Skitty ran into Torchic with a Tackle attack. Torchic slammed into Skitty with Quick Attack.

But the battle stopped when
Team Rocket burst into the room.
They were wearing silly costumes.

"Prepare for trouble!" James said. Jessie threw out her Seviper. "Seviper, use Haze!" she said. Black smoke came out of Seviper's mouth. The smoke filled the room.

Skitty got lost in the smoke. It ran over to Meowth.

"I think I am in love," said Meowth. "This is the cutest Pokémon I have ever seen!"

Jessie and James stole bottles of the healing mixes. They stuffed them into big bags.

Brock tackled James. The bottles in his bag broke. The smell from the bottles filled the air. Everyone started to cough.

Team Rocket ran
back to their balloon.
Ash and his friends
chased after them.
Brock grabbed the bag
from James.
"Get it back!" Jessie
told Seviper.
Ash threw out
his Corphish.

Wham! Corphish blasted Seviper with Bubblebeam. So James sent out Cacnea.

Bam! Corphish used its Crabhammer attack. Team Rocket fell into the balloon.

Then Ash called on his Taillow. It pecked a hole in the balloon. Team Rocket blasted off again!

"Is everybody okay?" Eliza asked.

"Yes," Brock said. "But I could only save this one bag!"

May ran up to them. "I cannot find Skitty anywhere!"

Not far away, Team Rocket's balloon crashed. They still had one bag left that they had stolen.

"At least we got what I wanted," said Jessie.

She opened the bag. Skitty popped out!

"What is that?" Jessie asked.

"It must belong to those twerps," James answered.

"Skitty is so cute!" Jessie said. "I am going to keep it!"

Meowth did not want Jessie
to keep Skitty! He imagined Skitty
blasting off over and over again with
Team Rocket.

"That is no kind of life for a
cute little Pokémon," Meowth said.

"Let me take Skitty for a drink of water," Meowth said to Jessie. He walked Skitty away from Jessie and James.

They came to a stream. "You have to go now!" Meowth told Skitty. Meowth threw a rock far away. Skitty ran after it.

Ash and May were still looking
for Skitty. Ash sent Taillow to look
from the skies. Taillow led them to
Team Rocket's crashed balloon.
"Skitty!" called May.

Eliza called on her Oddish. "Quick, Oddish, use your Sweet Scent!"

The smell filled the air. Pikachu began to dance happily.

"No Pokémon can resist Sweet Scent," Brock said.

Meowth and Wobbuffet sniffed the air. Then they ran after the wonderful smell.

Jessie and James chased after their Pokémon. They ran right into Ash and his friends!

"What did you do with my
Skitty?" May asked.
    "It is my Skitty!" Jessie said.
Just then Skitty walked up.

Jessie called on Dustox. May
called on Beautifly.

"Use Gust!" May said.

Beautifly blew Dustox away.
It smashed right into Team Rocket.

Pikachu used Thunderbolt.
Team Rocket blasted off—for the
second time!

"Are you okay, Skitty?" May asked. Skitty nodded.

"Then it is time for me to catch you!" May said. She started to throw her Poké Ball, but dropped it instead.

Skitty chased after it. The Poké Ball opened. Skitty went inside!

May and the others thanked Eliza and left. Skitty popped out of its Poké Ball.

"It let itself out!" May said, surprised.

Skitty chased its tail.

May laughed. "I love my new Skitty!" she said.

Who's That **Normal** Pokémon?

See page 45 or your *Normal Pokédex* for the answer.

Know Your Type

Two of these Pokémon are Normal Pokémon. One is not. Can you tell which one is not a Normal Type?

1.

Chansey™   Eevee™   Psyduck™

2.

Scyther™   Kecleon™   Lickitung™

3.

Azurill™   Azumarill™   Dunsparce™

4.		
Furret™	Golbat™	Porygon™

5.		
Slowking™	Teddiursa™	Spinda™

6.		
Mew™	Jigglypuff™	Snubbull™

7.		
Kangaskhan™	Tauros™	Phanpy™

Check page 45, your *Ultimate Sticker Book,* or your *Normal Pokédex* for the answers.

Think Pink!

These Pokémon are shown in black and white. One of the Pokémon in each row is really pink. Can you pick out the pink Pokémon in each row?

1.		
Cleffa™	Teddiursa™	Aipom™

2.		
Taillow™	Skitty™	Slakoth™

3.		
Castform™	Kecleon™	Snubbull™

Swablu™ Blissey™ Whismur™

Snorlax™ Wigglytuff™ Ursaring™

Vigoroth™ Lickitung™ Pidgey™

Miltank™ Granbull™ Hoothoot™

Check page 45 or your
Normal Pokédex for the answers.

Which Pokémon Doesn't Belong?

Two of the Normal Types in each row are related by Evolution. One is not. Can you pick out which Pokémon is *not* related?

1.

Clefairy™   Igglybuff™   Clefable™

2.

Skitty™   Meowth™   Persian™

3.

Linoone™   Zangoose™   Zigzagoon™

4.

Spearow™   Fearow™   Farfetch'd™

5.

Loudred™   Slaking™   Exploud™

6.

Castform™   Togetic™   Togepi™

7.

Raticate™   Rattata™   Sentret™

Check page 45, your *Ultimate Sticker Book,* or your *Normal Pokédex* for the answers.

Normal Pokémon Jokes

Why does Persian think it is the best Pokémon?

Because it is purr-fect!

How does Snubbull turn off the VCR?

It hits the paws button!

Why did May give the Teddiursa a coat?

Because she thought it looked a little bare!

Why did the Miltank go to Hollywood?

Because it wanted to be a moo-vie star!

What do you call a sleeping Tauros?

A bulldozer!

Why did Misty take Togepi to the beach?

Because she likes her eggs sunny-side up!

Answers

Page 37: Who's That Normal Pokémon?
Aipom!

Pages 38–39: Know Your Type
1. Psyduck (Water)
2. Scyther (Bug/Flying)
3. Azumarill (Water)
4. Golbat (Poison/Flying)
5. Slowking (Water/Psychic)
6. Mew (Psychic)
7. Phanpy (Ground)

Pages 40–41: Think Pink!
1. Cleffa
2. Skitty
3. Snubbull
4. Blissey
5. Wigglytuff
6. Lickitung
7. Miltank

Pages 42–43: Which Pokémon Doesn't Belong?
1. Igglybuff
2. Skitty
3. Zangoose
4. Farfetch'd
5. Slaking
6. Castform
7. Sentret